Rosetta, Rosetta,
Sit by Me!

Rosetta, Rosetta, Sit by Me!

by Linda Walvoord

illustrated by Eric Velasquez

Marshall Cavendish

New York • London • Singapore

To Kristen and Bria Fassler
—L.W.

For Harvey Dinnerstein,
a dedicated artist and instructor, whose masterful drawings
and paintings have inspired me for over twenty years
—E.V.

Marshall Cavendish
99 White Plains Road
Tarrytown, NY 10591
www.marshallcavendish.com
Text copyright © 2004 by Linda Walvoord

Library of Congress Cataloging-in-Publication Data
Walvoord, Linda.
Rosetta, Rosetta, sit by me! / by Linda Walvoord ;
illustrations by Eric Velasquez.

p. cm.

Summary: In 1848, Rosetta, the nine-year-old daughter of abolitionist Frederick Douglass,
becomes the only Black student at Miss Tracy's Female Seminary in Rochester, New York, and
while the students are pleased she is there, the faculty is not. Includes facts about Frederick
and Rosetta's lives.
Includes bibliographical references.

ISBN 0–7614–5171–4

1. Sprague, Rosetta Douglass—Juvenile fiction. [1. Sprague, Rosetta Douglass—Fiction. 2.
Douglass, Frederick, 1818–1895—Fiction. 3. Segregation in education—Fiction. 4. Race rela-
tions—Fiction. 5. Schools—Fiction. 6. African Americans—Fiction. 7. New York (State)—
History—1775–1865—Fiction.] I. Velasquez, Eric, ill. II. Title.
PZ7.W1785Ro 2004
[Fic]—dc22
2004003522

The text of this book is set in New Century Schoolbook.
The illustrations are rendered in charcoal.
Book design by Adam Mietlowski
Printed in The United States of America
First edition
Marshall Cavendish chapter book, First edition
1 3 5 6 4 2

Contents

Chapter One

The First Day of School, September, 1848

Miss Tracy's Female Seminary wasn't far from our house, but it seemed very far to me. I had to walk there by myself. I was afraid, since all the other students would be white. Papa said not to be afraid of white people, and I was trying hard. *I can do this*, I told myself. *I can be brave. What's so hard about walking to school on a beautiful, sunny morning?*

Even though I was already nine years old, I had never attended a real school before. Now I had to go to school alone. Papa would have walked with me, but he was in Ohio giving a speech. Mama couldn't walk with me, either. She was not feeling well this morning, and, besides, I didn't want her to walk with me. People might stare at her dress and her red bandanna. They might point at her and laugh. I didn't want my mama to have to see that. Anyway, Mama didn't want me to go to this school or any school.

I knew the way perfectly. Only a few weeks before, in August, Papa had taken me down Alexander Street. He had held my hand as we walked to Miss Tracy's fancy seminary. After talking to the principal, Miss Tracy, he had enrolled me. I had taken a test and passed it, showing I was ready.

There's nothing to be afraid of, I told myself, as I strolled under the shady trees that lined the street. Painted houses with big lawns and flower beds spread out around me. I turned the corner, knowing Papa had paid the school tuition money. They knew I was coming.

I hoped girls my age would be in my classes. It was a little shameful I hadn't been to a school before. That was Mama's decision when I was six and seven. Those were the years that Papa was away giving speeches in England. He sailed there after his first book was published. The book told right out what his old slave name was, and where he lived, and who his master was. Reading all of that, his former master might have found him and dragged him back into slavery. Papa's friends wanted to keep him safe. They persuaded him to flee across the ocean to England and live there for a while. Mama and my brothers and I stayed at home in America, in New Bedford, Massachusetts.

Chapter Two

Mama and Papa

During those two years in Massachusetts, when Papa was away, we lived in a little house. Mama worked for a shoe factory nearby in Lynn. She kept me at home to help with my little baby brothers—Charles, Lewis, and Frederick. She would bring armloads of leather and shoe forms into the house. The shoe forms were shaped like different-sized feet, to make larger and smaller shoes. Mama sat by the window sewing the leather. The factory man also brought a special sewing machine. As Mama used this on the shoes, I made lunch and kept the little boys busy. Mama worked for days. Then she took the finished shoes back to the factory and got her pay. She also got money from the sale of Papa's book, while he was away. Sometimes

Papa sent us money from his lectures in England. He also sent us letters. Friends had to come and read them to us. I wanted to learn to read and write so I could read Papa's letters, too.

Mama kept an account book in a drawer and saved every dollar she could. Although she could not read words, she could keep a bank account and was very thrifty. In fact, she was so thrifty that she made all the rugs and curtains in our house.

While we lived in New Bedford, sometimes a Quaker lady came to our house. She helped me learn to read, so I learned a little that way. But Mama needed my help, so she kept me out of school.

When Papa came back from England, he threw his arms around me and my little brothers. He had missed us terribly. He was very sorry I had not been to school. He wanted teachers to help me with reading every day. He wanted other children to become my friends, including white children. He told Mama he wanted me in a real school, and I would go to the best one. Sometimes I heard them argue quietly about it after I was supposed to be asleep.

The next winter, when I was eight, Papa insisted I go away to live with Miss Abigail Mott and Miss Lydia Mott, some Quaker ladies in Albany, New York. They would help me catch up with children my age who went to school. I lived with Miss Lydia and Miss Abigail for several months. My room was quiet. Several other children, both black and

white, came to their house every day for lessons. Mama begged to have me come back home, and in the spring, Papa agreed. In April we moved from New Bedford to Rochester, New York. Papa looked into my going to public school, but he was told I could only go to the colored school on the other side of town. I wouldn't be allowed to go to the public school in our own neighborhood, which was all-white. That's why he had me take the entrance test for Miss Tracy's.

In Rochester, Papa had a great, black, powerful printing press. He was the most famous runaway slave in America. He was the only Negro writer to own a newspaper, *The North Star*, in the whole nation. It was published in Rochester and mailed all over the country. People knew our family wherever we went. But what would the white girls say to me this morning, when they saw me coming to their school?

Today, for my first day, I polished my shoes twice. I braided my hair three different ways. My mother ironed my blouse and skirt. Fine-looking carriages were bringing the white girls to school. These girls wore

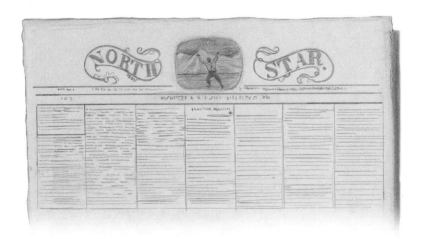

Two different front pages from The North Star, *top is circa 1848, bottom is circa 1858.*

pinafores and beautiful hair bows. They watched me climbing toward the door.

"We heard you were coming!" said one girl with red hair.

"Are you really going to be with us? Come play with us at recess," said another girl.

I was too shy to answer. Was it possible? Was I going to be happy?

I continued to climb the steps.

Chapter Three

All Alone

I found the principal's office inside. Miss Tracy was a plain looking lady. "I see you made it all right, Rosetta," she said. "Just follow this teacher."

The teacher led me down the hallway. Girls looked out of a classroom with big windows as we passed by. The teacher opened the door to a quiet, empty classroom. Nobody was there. She pointed to a desk and gave me several books. "You will study these," she said. Then she left me.

The room smelled of chalk and wax from the floor. I sat down, feeling butterflies the size of turtles in my stomach. The teacher had left before I could think of anything to say. There had been no time to ask her anything.

At first I sat very quietly. Surely someone else would come soon. Surely I would have only a little wait until they put me in a classroom with other girls. Maybe someone was talking about what class I should be in.

A long time passed. Did I misunderstand? No, I was sure I was doing just what

the teacher said. I didn't know what on earth to do. I decided I shouldn't go back to the principal's office. I certainly could not leave or go outside. I opened the books. They were very easy reading books. Because the Motts had taught me the letters and their sounds, I could read a little. But I was still feeling the butterflies.

After a long, long time, I heard the sound of feet. Girls were laughing in the halls as they got their coats. They clattered outside to the playground. It was recess time! Miss Lydia had explained that in a real school, the children go outside and play for a little while at *recess*. I wanted to run or jump rope or swing. My back and arms ached from sitting for so long.

A teacher came in.

"Will I go outside and play now?" I asked.

"No, Rosetta. I'm here to look at your work." She opened the book. "Do this page." I felt sad and ashamed. My first day at school was very, very hard. Papa hadn't said I would be all alone. But I didn't cry or argue. I just did the page.

When the recess was over and the school was full again, the teacher came back. She looked at my work. She nodded. "Very good. Now you may go outside. It's your turn to play."

"But everyone is finished. I won't have anyone to play with."

"Never mind that. This is your recess," said the teacher.

Under a big tree, I sat on the swing. I saw girls looking at me out the window, and one of them waved. Then a teacher came to the window. She motioned to the girls to sit down.

After a while I was called inside. I found the bathroom and got a drink of water. I looked at my blouse. It was wrinkled a little now, and my shoes were scuffed. Papa wanted me in this school to learn from good teachers and be with other children. He was a famous orator, had written a book, and was an editor of a newspaper. But he had never been to school a single day in his life. I was practically in prison! What would I tell Mama when I got home?

In my classroom I sat down again and lay my head on the desk to think. I couldn't tell Mama. If I told Mama, she would get mad at the school and would keep me home. If I told, I'd miss school until Papa returned from Ohio. He'd want me to go back, and I would have missed a lot. My stomach was tied up in knots. I knew already what I wanted to do. I wanted to wait for Papa. He wanted me to be brave. He would help me. He would be home in about two weeks.

Chapter Four

Waiting for Papa

Those two weeks were the longest days of my life. I did not cry to Mama or to anyone else. I went to school every day and sat alone in the same room. I went to recess alone and ate lunch alone. Nobody taught me. I heard the white girls chattering and laughing and doing their arithmetic. I used all the courage I had in me. I didn't run away. I didn't cry. I didn't disobey the teachers. And I didn't tell my mother what was happening. I waited for my father. I wanted to do what he expected.

I told myself all of Papa's favorite stories about when he was a boy. This made the time go faster. Papa had told me these stories many times. When he was a little slave boy in Maryland, he learned to read all by himself. His white mistress had started to help

him learn his letters. Then her husband stopped her, and she turned mean. She took all his books away, but he had kept on learning to read, all by himself. The only helpers he had were some friendly white boys he met in the streets of Baltimore. A few white workers in the shipyards where he played helped him, too. He had many friends in Baltimore who were colored. They encouraged him, but they couldn't help him because they couldn't read, either. Papa always knew that for colored people, there was a direct path from reading to freedom.

I had books—spelling books and pretty reading books with some pictures and easy words. Papa had never had any books as a boy. He had borrowed his mistress's Bible when she wasn't home. He used to sneak his young master, Tommy's, writing-practice books, too, tracing extra circles and strokes on the empty lines. Then he would put Tommy's writing books back, and no one ever noticed the extra writing. He found a few cast-off newspapers in the streets. The first real book he ever had was one that he bought himself for fifty cents. White boys

told him he should get a book named *The Columbian Orator*. It had great speeches in it. When he was twelve, he walked to a bookstore and bought it. He had earned the money to pay for it by shining shoes. But Papa in Baltimore as a slave had what I didn't have in this school—white friends! He had no idea that Miss Tracy didn't want white girls helping me or laughing with me or playing with me on the playground. Some people called my papa the Black Lion because he had a fiery voice and would speak out. If I could just be brave until he got back.

Chapter Five

Papa Goes to School

At last the day came when Papa returned. He burst inside the house with his suitcase and all his papers and packages. I ran to him and threw my arms around his neck. We all got big hugs and kisses from Papa. Then he took me on his knee and looked into my eyes. I knew the first thing that he would ask me. "How did it go in school, Rosetta?" His eyes sparkled, and he expected to hear happy news.

I couldn't hold back my tears anymore. I burst out crying. He looked amazed at this. "Why, Rosetta, darling, what on earth happened? What is it, child?" Mama came to the doorway, wiping her hands on her apron.

"They keep me all alone in a room by myself. No one teaches me. I'm all alone.

They won't let me play with the other girls at recess, and I even eat lunch all by myself. I am so lonely!" My misery came out and fell into his big arms.

"Who did this? Miss Tracy herself?"

"Yes, she made me sit alone the first day."

"Then we shall go together, tomorrow, you and I," he said.

Papa later wrote in his newspaper, "I was shocked, grieved, and indignant." He felt Miss Tracy had tricked us. She had taken Papa's money for tuition and then not let me into any of the classes. Now they had me in prison, in "solitary confinement," he wrote.

Every girl noticed when my tall, handsome father, Frederick Douglass, came with me to school the next day. We walked hand in hand up the steps to the principal's office. The great lion, Frederick Douglass, would face the little, sparrowlike Miss Tracy, with her small, pinched, sparrow face.

Chapter Six

The Children Help Out

"My daughter, Rosetta, says that she is being kept away from other pupils. Is this true?" Papa asked.

"Yes, it is," was the cool reply. "If I had done otherwise, it would have injured my school and its reputation."

"And how would that be?"

"Some of our families would object if she were in classes with their children. We are a private school, so we are obligated to observe the wishes of the parents."

"If you were going to exclude my daughter, you should have told me that in the beginning," he said. Papa's words fell like hammers. He reminded Miss Tracy he had paid tuition like the other parents. Papa sounded very firm. Not a trace of a slave's

accent remained in his voice. He sounded exactly like a senator or congressman.

Miss Tracy grew a bit flustered. "There would be opposition to your daughter sitting in the white classroom," she said.

"I don't believe that," said Papa. "Let us ask the students."

"Very well then, I will put the question to them. Come with me," said Miss Tracy.

To my surprise, Miss Tracy led us down the hallway. She knocked briefly on a door and faced the surprised teacher and students. Papa and I stepped into the silent room. Every paper was quiet. Every face was quiet. The fall sun streamed through the big windows. Some problems were written on the board. I looked at the faces of the white girls. No one looked uneasy. In fact, some of them smiled at me!

Miss Tracy rapped for attention. "Girls, Mr. Douglass is here to see if his daughter may be in this class," she said. "How many of you want Rosetta to be in your class? Raise your hands." She folded her arms.

The arm of every single girl shot into the air.

Miss Tracy thought the girls had misunderstood. "No, you did not understand. I said how many of you feel that Rosetta Douglass *should* be allowed to come into this class as a pupil?"

Again, every girl lifted her hand in the air.

"I do!"

"I do!" they called.

Miss Tracy grew more red faced and flustered. One by one she called on each of the girls.

One girl said she did not mind if I stayed.

"Did you mean to vote so? Are you accustomed to colored children?" Miss Tracy demanded.

The girl did not answer.

"Where would she sit, then?" demanded Miss Tracy.

The girls started to compete. "Next to me!"

"No, let her sit here!" came another voice.

"Rosetta, sit by me! Sit by me!"

Other hands shot up eagerly.

"By me!"

Papa and I looked at each other and grinned. He had told me to trust white people! We would never forget that day. "The children's hearts were right," my father later wrote in a letter to Mark Twain.

Miss Tracy soon recovered. "Well, we are not finished with this subject!" she said.

Chapter Seven

Mr. Warner Objects

That was my last day at Miss Tracy's school, but I didn't know it at the time. The children wanted me, but Miss Tracy wasn't finished. I could have been happy there. But this was 1848. So the story did not end.

That evening, without telling Papa or me, Miss Tracy called a parents' meeting. Parents crowded into the meeting room. Papa and I weren't there, but our friends later told us what happened. Miss Tracy asked how many parents agreed that they wanted me to enroll. All the hands went up, all except for the hand of one person.

"And who objects?" she asked.

Mr. Horatio G. Warner stood up. He was a powerful man. He was the editor of *The Rochester Courier*, a newspaper with a few hundred readers. Papa's paper, *The North Star*, which he had started just the year before, was sent all over the nation to thousands of readers. The newspaper published by Horatio G. Warner was local. Papa spoke to big crowds everywhere in the North, and he traveled and wrote books. Mr. Warner was unknown outside of Rochester.

Mr. Warner cleared his throat. "I do not believe this enrollment is suitable, because it betrays the boundaries that society and nature have set in place for the education of our youth," he said. Then he launched into a long speech. Mr. Warner didn't want his

daughter to go to school with the daughter of Frederick Douglass. He acted like my father was a paid-abolitionist rabble-rouser and troublemaker. He said Papa was not really from this city. He had lately come from another state to bother the good citizens of this town. He went on like that.

After Mr. Warner's long speech, Miss Tracy took another vote of the parents. Again, all the parents except Mr. Warner voted to have me come to Miss Tracy's Female Seminary. But by Miss Tracy's rules, Mr. Warner won. "If there were no objection, I would allow this enrollment," said Miss Tracy. "But since there is one objection, Rosetta will not be allowed. I am a good Christian, and I oppose slavery. But the issue before us is another one altogether. I am responsible for a safe, peaceful environment, and this is a threat to our peace."

Chapter Eight

I Leave School

While Miss Tracy's secret meeting was going on, Papa and I were at home explaining to Mama what a wonderful thing had happened. We thought I was in the school. So the next morning, I walked to school as usual with my books under my arm. This time I could hardly wait.

But when I reached the steps, Miss Tracy met me there. She must have been watching for me out the window. "Rosetta, you are no longer a student here. Please return home."

For a moment I just stood there. I didn't understand. She had to tell me twice to go back home.

I fled so fast that no one could see the tears of shame stinging my eyes. Somehow I made it home without dropping my books.

I rushed inside, hardly able to breathe. This time I told Mama just what had happened.

"I knew it," she said. "I knew this would come to grief." She sent a boy from the neighborhood to get Papa from his office. He came rushing home, but by then I had dried my tears and was playing with Lewis and Charles. "Will you stay home and play with us now, Rosetta?" my little brother Charles asked.

Papa came into the room and gave me a hug. "It's all right, Rosa. It's all right," he said. He called me Rosa sometimes at home.

"Will I go to the colored school now, Papa? Will I go where the school board wants me to go?"

"No, Rosetta. You will go to the best school we can find."

Mama looked sad. She hugged me. "I told you, Frederick, this child does not need to leave home. She needs protection in a home. This is too much turmoil for her young heart."

"Rosetta, are you brave?" He looked me in the eyes. This time he used my grown-up name.

"Yes, Papa."

"Do you want to have the very best teachers you could have?"

"Yes, Papa."

"Well then, it is settled," he said. "I'll send a telegram, and then we shall see."

While he was gone, Mama talked to me in the kitchen. "Reading is not the most important thing," she said. "My life is happy, but I don't know how to read. You know your father has tried to teach me. I can't learn. I am happy without reading."

"But I know how to read a little already, Mama. In the future, colored children will *have* to learn."

"I know, I know, the world is changing. But I want you at home, where they cannot hurt you."

"Mama, the white girls wanted me. They liked me. I know they did. They even voted against their teachers in order to take me into their class."

"I know that. I know that."

"I want to play with them. Wait till they see me jump rope."

"You are a brave girl."

Chapter Nine

Off to Albany

So Mama's dream that I would never be hurt and Papa's dream that I would make my way in the world were in conflict. Papa sent off a telegram. That afternoon I was so restless that finally Mama let me go down to the newspaper office to find Papa. I helped him set type. He showed me how to put the sticks of letters into the trays just straight. Then he showed me how to lock them in the pages. It was inky and dirty and exciting. I loved being around his office. Mr. Delaney was there, too, talking about articles and taking notes as Papa wrote.

Soon a telegraph message arrived for Papa. A messenger in a uniform came to the office to deliver it. I watched as he handed my father the paper. Papa read it slowly, and a smile crossed his face. He showed it to Mr. Delaney.

"How shall she learn if she's not taught properly?" Mr. Delaney asked. "The Mott sisters are an excellent choice."

"Rosetta," said Papa. "I have made some new arrangements. Miss Abigail answered my telegram instantly. You will go to Albany. The Motts will be happy to have you live with them again, so that you can go to their school."

"Albany is so far from here," I said.

"Thats right. Two hundred and twenty-five miles. I will take you on the evening train." He sent a messenger to Mama, asking her to get my clothes ready. There was no time to waste. The school year had started, and he didn't want me to fall behind.

Later my father would write a public letter in his newspaper. It would be addressed to Mr. Warner. It would explain that after Miss Tracy sent me home, I was welcomed into another school with white children. He pointed out that this happened within five hours of my being sent home from Miss Tracy's. That meant Papa had rushed to the telegraph office and heard back from Albany, all in one day. He didn't mention, in his letter to Mr. Warner, that my new school was over two hundred miles away!

We had a farewell dinner. Mama brought my favorite chicken and squash and mashed potatoes to the table. I almost cried, but I was excited, too. Papa made my journey sound like an adventure. He traveled on the great, huffing railway locomotives all the time, and thousands of people listened to his speeches. Tonight I would leave my pretty room, with the curtains Mama had made herself, and my soft bed, and my mama and little brothers. Papa and I would go down to the railway station, and we would board the train as it stood in the station in a cloud of white smoke. All night we would sit in the velvet seats and watch the night sky. I would leave my family and study with other children who were strangers. It was that important for me to learn to read, and do arithmetic, and have good teachers. All because of Mr. Horatio G. Warner!

"I'll wrap you some apples and cheese for the train," Mama said.

She had washed and ironed all my clothes, and they were perfect. She folded them into a big valise. Then she gave me gloves and a hat to wear. "You be proper and polite, Rosetta, and help the sisters with the work. You're not a royal princess."

"They have always treated you well," Papa said. Carrying my valise, Papa helped me climb into the train. Then he climbed on after me.

"All aboard!" the conductor shouted, waving his lantern.

That night I watched the rolling fields and hills and looked at the stars. We did not sleep. I thought about how much my life had changed in one year. And tonight before I'd left, Mama had told me some special news. Next spring, she'd said, she would have another baby! I hoped for a baby girl this time since I already had three little brothers.

In the morning the two ladies I remembered, Miss Lydia and Miss Abigail, met us with a horse and buggy. We had a meal together. Later that day Papa said good-bye before boarding the train for home.

"I will write you often," he promised and hugged me good-bye.

For the whole winter, I lived with Miss Abigail and Miss Lydia. Even though I had a little room all my own, with a pretty quilt on the bed, I was lonesome for my family. But I knew I was doing the right thing. I traveled home by train at Christmas and then returned

again to Albany to continue my lessons.

A Quaker home is very plain. In my room there were no frills or ruffles, no bright colors, no dolls or pretty toys. But I did learn to love reading, and I had lots of books and other children to play with every day. The Mott sisters had a cousin in Philadelphia named James Mott. His wife, Lucretia, sometimes visited. She was a good friend of Papa's, and she was a writer and speaker for women's rights. Papa said that women should vote! We would sit and drink tea and talk about all that women would do one day in this big world. Including me!

I was proud that before long, when Papa sent letters, I could read them myself. I started writing letters to Papa, too. I knew that I would be writing letters to him for the rest of my life. Busy as he was, he always wrote back. In March he sent news that I had a new baby sister named Annie. I missed Mama. With a new baby, she needed my help. By spring the Mott sisters thought I had learned enough to go home early. I thanked them for helping me and waved good-bye. I arrived home and threw my arms around Mama, Papa, my brothers, and my brand-new baby sister.

Chapter Ten

Papa Fights Back

While I had been away, Papa had not let up on Mr. Warner or the Rochester schools. Beginning in the fall when I had left for Albany, Papa blasted Mr. Warner in the press. He used his pen like a sword, fighting with words. He wanted to get the all-white public schools of Rochester, New York, to accept colored children who lived nearby. My papa wrote that when a person had acted unjustly, he did not have a right to privacy. "The public have a right to ferret them out, and bring their conduct before . . . the country for investigation," he wrote. He wanted the American public to read about Mr. Warner's behavior. When he told my story in *The North Star*, readers both black and white read about me. Far away in Springfield, Illinois, even a young, unknown lawyer named

Abraham Lincoln was reading *The North Star*. My lonely two weeks at Miss Tracy's Female Seminary were known all over the land. Papa wrote this to Mr. Warner: "We differ in color, it is true . . . but who is to decide which color is more pleasing to God, or most honorable among men? But I do not wish to waste words or argument on one who . . . has shown himself full of pride and prejudice." He called Mr. Warner "a despised minority of one," since Mr. Warner was the only parent who had objected to my attending Miss Tracy's.

Papa did not just blast out words in one letter. He kept up the pressure. Every year after 1848 he asked the Rochester School Board for special meetings. He asked them to reconsider the question of how to educate his children. Each year they kept saying no, they would not allow his children to attend the local public school in our neighborhood. "But I pay the taxes on my home, like every other homeowner," Papa replied. Still, they kept saying no. Papa made fiery speeches. Like a dripping faucet, he repeated his goals again and again and again. He kept writing about the news story in his paper. "Right is of no sex—truth is of no color—God is the father of us all, and we are brethren" was the paper's motto.

Papa not only used his pen to fight for equal schooling for colored and white children. He also used other means to fight for equality between the two races. When I was a baby in Massachusetts and he was starting to travel and give speeches, he would refuse to sit in the colored seats on trains. He always took a seat in the white section. Some conductors tried to remove him from the train, but my papa hung onto his seat. He was so strong that it took six men to lift him up, seat and all, and throw him off.

While he sat on a nice, soft seat on the ground, the railroad had to order a new chair. The next week he would start his protest again. After a while, the railroad company ordered the train not to stop in our town at all. The railroad people were worried that Frederick Douglass would keep getting on. He embarrassed the people who showed prejudice. He believed that shame is a powerful feeling. He always had so many stories. Sometimes my family laughed and sometimes we cried at how hard he worked to make a way for us.

Chapter Eleven

Good News!

When I moved back to Rochester, Papa hired a private tutor, Miss Phebe Thayer, to come to the house each day. Charles, Lewis, Frederick, and I sat and worked with Miss Thayer. My baby sister, Annie, toddled about and watched us. Annie chewed on pencils and made marks on her own papers on the floor. Helping my little brothers and sister, I began to think I'd like to be a teacher one day.

Eventually I outgrew Miss Thayer's home school. Papa sent me on the train once more, this time to Ohio. In 1854, when I was fifteen, I attended Oberlin College. I studied to become a teacher in the Young Ladies' Preparatory Department. At that time Oberlin was one of the only

colleges that would accept women. I studied there for a term, then left to become a teacher in Philadelphia. After another year or two, I moved to Salem, New Jersey, where I passed the exams to become a licensed teacher.

In New Jersey I taught school to working people. My students worked during the daytime as gardeners, maids, and cooks. At night they came to my school to learn arithmetic, geography, and history.

In Philadelphia and later in New Jersey, I boarded with close friends or relatives of my parents. In Salem, my relatives, Uncle Perry and Aunt Lizzie, were so poor that I often skipped dinner to save them the expense. I bought my own candles and soap with money my papa sent me. One day in 1857, I went home for a visit. My father flew into the coffee shop where I was talking with friends. "Rosetta! Rosetta! We've done it! We've won! The Rochester Public School Board is going to let Annie enter our local school for first grade. Segregation is over in Rochester!"

NORTH STAR

1857

SCHOOL SEGREGATION IS OUTLAWED IN ROCHESTER

Good News!

I saw the tears in Papa's eyes. Nine years of steady protests had made a difference. Now my baby sister could walk to public school happily under the trees in our neighborhood. There would be no tuition, no angry Mr. Warner to make her go back home. All of Papa's hard work had finally paid off.

Chapter Twelve

Say Hello to the Future

At the time Annie started school, there was a lot of talk about how a war was coming. The North and South had been arguing bitterly about whether slavery should exist in the new states that were coming into the Union. My father continued to speak out against slavery and to ask for equal freedom for Negroes and whites. But in 1859, Papa faced a dangerous time. A white man named John Brown led an attack on a federal fort in Harper's Ferry, Virginia, hoping to start a slave rebellion. The U.S. Army quickly took control of the fort, and John Brown was executed. There were rumors that Papa had helped John Brown. To escape danger, Papa sailed again to England. While he was there, a tragedy struck our home. Annie got sick with scarlet fever and, at age eleven, died. We sent a telegraph to Papa with news of her death. With a heavy heart, he sailed home on the next ship. He arrived too late for her funeral.

After Annie's death, we were still proud of my little sister. Annie had been one of the first Negro children in the North to go to public school with white children. We visited Annie's grave for the rest of our lives.

In 1861, war finally broke out. Papa recruited colored soldiers to fight for the Union. My two brothers, Charles and Lewis, fought. It was during this time that I met a Union soldier named Nathan Sprague. We became engaged and married in 1863.

As the war continued, my father worked for equal treatment for colored and white soldiers. He met with Abraham Lincoln several times.

Shortly after the war ended, Nathan and I settled in the Rochester area. For a time, we lived in my parents' home and began raising our own family. One terrible night in 1872, when we were living with

Mama in the house in Rochester and Papa was away, I woke to the smell of smoke. Our house burned down that night. It was a great loss, since so many memories were part of that house.

Sometimes I still go to my father's office, helping with his mail and checking the proofs of his new writings. As I work on the newspaper's printing, I cross my fingers and think about my little sister, Annie. Maybe the future will fulfill my father's dream. Maybe more white children will raise their hands for freedom. I hope white and black children will go to school together, and all of them will be free. Sometimes children see the truth that adults refuse to look at. The girls in Miss Tracy's Female Seminary were saying hello to the future, as they called out that day, "Rosetta, Rosetta, sit by me!"

More About Frederick
and Rosetta Douglass

Frederick Douglass was born in 1818 in a poor region on Maryland's Eastern Shore. His mother, Harriet Bailey, was a house slave who belonged to a plantation manager named Aaron Anthony. Douglass later wrote, "My father was a white man . . . . The opinion was also whispered that my master was my father," though he was never sure if this master was Captain Aaron Anthony, Thomas Auld (a later owner), or some other white man. Harriet named the baby Frederick Augustus Washington Bailey. Soon after his birth, she was sent to a distant farm to work in the fields and could no longer care for her infant.

Frederick grew up in the care of his grandma Betsy Bailey. She lived in a cabin seventeen miles from the Anthony household. If his mother, Harriet, wanted to see "Freddie," she had to walk all night to reach Grandma Bailey's cabin and return to the fields to start work the next day.

Frederick's grandmother caught fish and grew vegetables to feed the five or six children placed in her care. Her husband, Isaac Bailey, was a free man who worked for pay. When Frederick was about six, Betsy was ordered to take him to the plantation where Master Anthony managed a large number of slaves. Anthony was employed by Colonel Edward Lloyd, a rich man and the former governor of Maryland. The colonel owned about 1,000 slaves spread across twenty-three farms. Anthony owned three farms, and he rented out most of the thirty slaves that he owned. Later Douglass wrote that slave children who arrived for training at the plantation were thought of "like so many pigs." They ate corn mush from a pig trough, which they scooped out with their hands.

Frederick was often cold, as he was given only one thin, linen shirt each year to cover him. He had no pants or shoes until he was about nine years old. "My feet have been so cracked with the frost, that the pen with which I am writing might be laid in the gashes," he wrote.

When Frederick was nine, Captain Anthony gave permission to his daughter, Lucretia Anthony, to send Frederick to work in the city of Baltimore. Lucretia did not yet own Frederick, but she hoped that after her father passed away she would. In the meantime, she and her fiancé, Thomas Auld, thought "Freddie" should gain some work experience in Baltimore. They loaned him to Lucretia's fiancé's brother, Hugh Auld, and his wife, Sophia. In their home, Freddie would help take care of the Auld's two-year-old child, Tommie.

Frederick's new position was an important turning point in his life. Lucretia's husband-to-be, Thomas, and his brother, Hugh Auld, were involved in shipbuilding. They wanted to train Frederick to some day work on the docks. By doing that, he'd take in more money for the family than if they rented him out as a slave in the country.

Colonel Lloyd owned a fancy yacht which often sailed to Baltimore, and Thomas Auld was its captain. Thus Frederick reached his new home by boat.

While living in the city, Frederick slept in a real bed and was given pants and shoes to wear. He also used a table and a chair for the first time and met people who could read. He played in the streets with white boys who went to school, and he attended a church where he heard Bible stories and hymns. Gradually, with the help of Mrs. Hugh Auld and a few of his street friends, he learned to read and write. Freddie's white mistress taught him the alphabet, but then her husband put a stop to it. From then on, Douglass was on his own.

One day Frederick's white playmates told him about a book of great speeches called *The Columbian Orator*. They said it contained a story about a slave who won an argument with his white master. Frederick was impressed and walked a long way to a bookstore. With fifty cents that he had earned shining shoes, he bought a copy of *The Columbian Orator*. He was excited by some of the ideas in the book, including those about liberty, democracy, and courage.

A few years later, Aaron Anthony died, and Lucretia inherited Frederick, just as she had hoped. But very soon she died, too, and her husband, Thomas Auld, became Douglass's owner. Thomas then remarried, and his new wife, Rowena Auld, persuaded Thomas to order Frederick back to the country. Frederick was then sixteen. He was a literate, troubled slave who deeply resented his master. Auld, now a storekeeper, rented him out to work in the fields for different farmers. After his years in Baltimore, Douglass was miserable in the country. With four friends, he tried to escape but was caught and sent to jail. When he was released, Thomas Auld sent him back to Baltimore. Once again, Frederick lived with Thomas's brother, Hugh, and his wife, Sophia. This time, however, he would earn money by working in the shipyards, then turn his wages over to the Aulds.

While working in Baltimore, Douglass met Anna Murray, his future bride. Anna was free, so she was allowed to marry. Frederick, as a slave, could not marry since it was against the law. Douglass knew he could earn as much as any white man on the docks, and he wanted to marry Anna. For these two reasons, he decided to run away to the North, where he hoped he could become free.

Douglass was twenty when he left for New York, a state where no one owned slaves. On September, 3, 1838, he arrived in New York City. As soon as he found a place to stay, he wrote to Anna. She came north by train, and soon they got married. Friends advised them to move to New Bedford, Massachusetts, a Quaker town, where they would be welcome.

Rosetta was born on June 24, 1839. Her younger brothers, Charles, Lewis, and Frederick, were born in 1840, 1842, and 1844.

In the North, Douglass made a name for himself by lecturing on the horrors of slavery. He was such a good speaker that he could hold an audience's attention for up to two hours. William Lloyd Garrison, a leading white abolitionist, heard him speak in 1841. He was impressed by Douglass's passion, wit, and powerful voice. Garrison offered him a steady job lecturing for the Massachusetts Anti-Slavery Society. For the next four years, Douglass crisscrossed New England, giving speeches. But because he did not reveal the name of his master or where he had been a slave, some people did not believe his story.

In 1845 Douglass wrote his first book, *Narrative of the Life of Frederick Douglass, Written By Himself*. He told the full story of his life, including names, dates, and places. News of the book swept across the country. Thousands of copies were sold. Since Douglass's book included details of his recent life as a slave, however, he was in danger of being recaptured by his former master, Thomas Auld. He took the advice of friends and fled to England, where he would be safe. There he lectured and traveled, preaching against slavery, for almost two years.

Anna and the children stayed behind in Massachusetts. Because Anna had never been a slave, she was not in danger of being recaptured. She worked for a shoe factory to support the family. Rosetta turned six, then seven and eight while her father was away.

During Douglass's absence from 1845 to 1847, English Quaker abolitionists bargained with Thomas Auld. They tried to buy Frederick's life, and a sale was finally arranged. Quakers paid Auld $710.96. Auld signed his former slave's free papers in December 1846. The next spring, free papers in hand, Douglass returned to America to continue his work. He was no longer just a runaway slave who could be recaptured. He was a free man.

When he arrived home, the Douglass family was happy to be together again. But Frederick was surprised and upset to find that Rosetta had not been attending school. During the fall and winter of 1847-48, he arranged for her to be tutored by two white sisters, Abigail and Lydia Mott, who lived in Albany, New York. Meanwhile, he moved his family from Massachusetts to Rochester, New York, where he planned to start a newspaper, *The North Star*.

THE NORTH STAR.

VOL. I. NO. 38.   ROCHESTER, N. Y., FRIDAY, SEPTEMBER 15, 1848.   WHOLE NO.—38.

Selections.

THE POLICY OF SLAVERY.

While living with the Motts in Albany, Rosetta learned to read and write well for her age. As a result, Douglass decided she should return home and attend public school in Rochester. New Bedford, the Quaker town where the Douglasses first lived, had had integrated schools. But Rochester's public schools were different. When Douglass tried to enroll Rosetta for fall, 1848, the city refused to allow her to attend the public school in the white neighborhood where the Douglasses lived. Instead they said she was to go to a "colored" public school across town. Douglass then enrolled her in Miss Tracy's Female Seminary, a private white girls' school near the Douglass home. On the first day of school, Rosetta was "sent" there (Douglass's wording) and must have been surprised and hurt to find that no one took her to the regular school classroom. She was put in a room by herself. Her father was away at the time, but when he returned and found out what had happened, he was shocked and angry.

Douglass wrote about Rosetta's painful experience at Miss Tracy's in *The North Star*. In an angry letter addressed to H. G. Warner, a white parent who had objected to Rosetta's presence at Miss Tracy's, Douglass re-told Rosetta's story. He hoped his letter, when printed in the newspaper, would shame the city into integrating its public schools.

Douglass also used his newspaper as a means to attack Thomas Auld and other slaveholders. Thomas Auld was never a rich man. In about 1828, while Freddie was in Baltimore, Auld had lost his job as a captain for Colonel Lloyd. Next he failed as a shipbuilder and later as a storekeeper. But as he put Frederick to

work, first in the countryside and then in the Baltimore shipyards, Auld pocketed more than $2,200 from his slave's work (his own salary as a captain had been only $20 a month). No wonder Douglass felt that he had been directly robbed by a "mean" master.

Douglass fought for other rights, too, such as the right of women to vote. In 1848 he took a stand for women's rights when he attended the first women's rights convention in Seneca Falls, New York. He urged women to demand the right to vote. And he continued to work for black and white people to be educated together as equals.

By 1853 the Rochester school system had improved its "colored schools" by hiring better teachers and repairing its buildings. Rosetta and her brothers, Charles and Lewis, attended the all-black District 13 Public School that year. In 1855 Douglass wrote his second book, *My Bondage and My Freedom*. His days became even busier with lecture tours, his newspaper, and the need to raise subscriptions to support its weekly costs, about eighty dollars a week. Often Rosetta and the boys helped their father by setting type and doing errands in the print shop. On the masthead, Douglass placed his motto: "Right is of no sex—Truth is of no color—God is the Father of us all, and we are all Brethren."

Finally, in 1857, the Rochester Public Schools gave in to Douglass's demands and ruled that Annie could attend her local "all-white" public school.

As Douglass grew older, his position on slavery began to shift. He no longer agreed with William Lloyd Garrison's views that slavery could be abolished by peaceful means. In 1859 the white abolitionist leader John Brown urged Douglass to support his plans for a violent slave revolt in the Virginia town of Harper's Ferry. Douglass refused to support the attack. He knew it would be hopeless and would enrage most Americans. But in desperate times he felt slaves would revolt, and he considered John Brown a great leader, calling him a "noble old hero." On October 16, 1859, with a small band of black and white volunteers, Brown attacked Harper's Ferry. Brown and his men seized guns and ammunition. The next night General Robert E. Lee and his troops stormed Brown's small band. Brown was captured, found guilty of treason, and hanged two months later. The governor of Virginia thought Douglass was involved and asked a judge to order his arrest. Douglass quickly fled the country. He again sailed to England for a lecture tour.

In 1860, while in England, he received news that his youngest daughter, Annie, had died at age eleven. Douglass rushed home to grieve with his family. Once again he felt safe, as the accusations against him had long since disappeared.

Back in the United States, Douglass got involved with the Underground Railroad. He and Anna offered safety to many runaway slaves who traveled secretly through New York on their way to Canada. The Douglass's hid more than 400 slaves during the 1850s, including some led by Harriet Tubman.

At this time, Rosetta decided she wanted to further her education. In 1854 she boarded a train for Oberlin College in Ohio. She enrolled in the Young Ladies' Preparatory Department to train as a teacher. After a year of study, she taught in Philadelphia and later in Salem, New Jersey. She lived with family friends or relatives in each place. Her life as a single woman was not easy. The pathway to success for an unmarried, black woman was narrow and difficult. In Salem she studied at Salem Normal School by day. At night she taught working people after they finished their day jobs. Rosetta taught them to read and write. She encouraged them to dream of a bright future for themselves and for their children.

During the Civil War, Rosetta fell in love with an officer, Nathan Sprague, and they married in 1863. Nathan was a soldier whose father had been a runaway slave. Scholar William S. McFeely says, "In Nathan, the feistiness of the runaway did not translate into talent. He proved as inept as her father was able. But like her mother, once married, Rosetta never gave up on her man."

The coming of the Civil War brought Frederick Douglass to the forefront of politics. In the election of 1860, Douglass backed Gerrit Smith, an antislavery candidate. But when he realized that Smith's chances for election were slim, he switched his support to Abraham Lincoln. The Democratic Party was divided between two candidates, so Lincoln, a Republican, won the election. As Southern states left the Union, both North and South prepared for war. In 1861 Douglass traveled throughout the Northern states. He urged black, young men to sign up for the Union army. Two of his own sons fought under Colonel Robert Shaw in the 54th Massachusetts.

Douglass met with Lincoln several times during the war. Once, he pleaded with the president to pay black soldiers the same wages that white soldiers received. Another time he offered to help win more secret support from the South. Lincoln asked Douglass to make a plan to lead slaves out of the South, in case a Northern victory seemed hopeless. By that time the war had cost so many lives, many people on both sides hated Lincoln and were weary of fighting. But Douglass was convinced that Lincoln was a friend of the slaves. Lincoln and Douglass's secret plan was never used, because the North won important victories in 1864. When General Sherman marched across the Southern states toward Richmond, Virginia, he left a path of destruction that forced the Southern states to surrender. These victories gave Lincoln the support he needed to win re-election in 1864.

After the bitter war, Douglass supported Lincoln's desire to heal the nation's wounds. But the path was hard. Once, Douglass approached the doors of the White House for Lincoln's inaugural celebration, an event to which Lincoln had invited him. Guards asked Douglass to leave. Hearing the news, Lincoln himself came to the door and asked the guards to step aside and let Frederick come in. "Here comes my friend, Douglass," said Lincoln, escorting Douglass by the arm.

Shortly after the war ended on April 9, 1865, Lincoln was assassinated. Douglass mourned the president's death. Yet not even that sorrow could erase his great joy that the war to end slavery had been won.

In 1872 Douglass decided to move his family from Rochester to Washington, D.C., the nation's capital. He needed a new home, since his Rochester home had burned to the ground that year. Rosetta, then thirty-three years old, had been living in her parents' home with her husband and family when the fire occurred. She had been the first to smell the smoke.

Some people suspected that the fire had been set by some of Douglass's enemies. All of Douglass's papers and many records of his work were lost in the flames.

Once in Washington, Douglass continued to try to improve the future of his people. He traveled across the country and saw that Negroes were banned from certain public places. They had neither fair trials nor equal education. He urged his people to do what they could. One of his most famous speeches, "The Self-Made Man," urged Negroes to seize every opportunity to improve their lives. Toward the end of his public career, Douglass served briefly as the U.S. Minister to Haiti.

As Douglass neared the age of 60, he began to slow down. He spent more time at Cedar Hill, a second house he had bought outside of Washington. It had twenty rooms and sat on fifteen acres. This residence still exists today as a memorial, as does his earlier home in Washington, near the Capitol. In 1881 he wrote his third autobiography and, in 1892, revised it again as *The Life and Times of Frederick Douglass*. He never stopped dreaming of full equality for blacks. Once, a young man asked him what he could do to advance the black race. The aging, white-haired Douglass replied simply, "Agitate, agitate, agitate." Throughout his life, he used his powerful voice and pen to support the cause of freedom.

Unlike her father's life, Rosetta's unfolded more quietly. Still, she shared his views on education, freedom, and equality. Nathan never held down a job for long. He worked as a gardener, taxi-carriage driver, and chicken farmer. Sadly he never earned enough money to support his family. To make ends meet, he and Rosetta and their children occasionally lived with Rosetta's parents. This was a great disappointment to Douglass.

Both Rosetta and Douglass were lonely at times. In 1869 Rosetta wrote to her father, "You say you are a lonely man, no one knows it better than myself and the causes. I have been in a measure lonely myself but would not allow myself to analyze my feelings as I was the daughter and had duties to fulfill in that relation. . . ." She added that as a child, her "position was anything but pleasant. You used often to say that we were all glad when you left, something that was so far from the truth as far as I was concerned. I never dared to show much zeal about anything where you were concerned, as I could never have ridicule." She added, "jealousy is one of the leading traits in our family." She loved her father but "could readily bring a storm about ears if I endorsed any of your sentiments about matters pertaining to the household. . . ." She often felt caught between her mother's values, in her home and family, and her father's bright dreams of achievement. She once wrote to him in 1862, ". . . I wish to be all you would have me be and I wish also to do some thing to make *mother* happy and if both were interested in the same pursuits it would be easier for me."

Sometimes Rosetta suffered from feeling that her father was not pleased with her. Once Douglass wrote that she was "all mouth and no hands." He bought her a sewing machine and encouraged her to sew for wages. She could not do much with it, however, because at that time she had two young children to care for. Rosetta's letters show that she grew closer to her father during the years she shared his letters with the rest of the family. She handled much of her father's mail from political correspondents and social friends. After her mother's death in 1881, Rosetta wrote and published a pamphlet of tribute to Anna Douglass called "My Mother as I Recall Her." The memorial pamphlet painted a loving picture of her mother, which seems at odds with the inner conflicts Rosetta expressed in her letters.

Douglass's path to his own education was tough. But Rosetta's struggle to gain an education and realize her hopes as a teacher, wife, mother, and leader was in many ways just as hard and equally lonely. In her lifelong concern with education, Rosetta often must have remembered her first days of school and the girls who raised their hands, calling out, "Rosetta, Rosetta, sit by me!"

Important Dates

February 14, 1818—Frederick Douglass's birth date, according to most scholars. He is named Frederick Augustus Washington Bailey and is soon separated from his mother.

1824—Frederick is sent to the Lloyd plantation, after living with his grandmother, Betsy Bailey. He spends about eighteen months on the plantation before being sent to work as a house slave in Baltimore for his new owners, the Aulds.

1826–7—He works as a companion to Hugh and Sophia Auld's young son.

1828—Aaron Anthony dies, and Lucretia Anthony Auld becomes Douglass's new owner. She dies, and Frederick's next owner becomes Lucretia's husband, Thomas Auld. He sends Douglass to Baltimore again.

1834—Auld orders Douglass back to the country, this time for two to three years. Frederick, now sixteen, is rented out to various farmers for wages.

1836—Frederick makes an escape plan with four friends. They are caught and arrested. Thomas Auld throws Douglass in jail before sending him back to Hugh and Sophia Auld's in Baltimore. Douglass works in the shipyards, giving his wages to the Aulds. He meets and falls in love with Anna Murray, a free woman.

September 3, 1838—Frederick's second escape attempt succeeds. He arrives in New York City without friends or money. Anna travels north to join him in New York, and they are married. They move to New Bedford, Massachusetts.

1838–41—The family lives in New Bedford and later moves to nearby Lynn, Massachusetts.

June 24, 1839—Rosetta is born.

1840—Lewis Henry Douglass is born.

1841—Frederick Douglass gives his first speech before a big white audience on Nantucket Island. William Lloyd Garrison hires him to work for the Massachusetts Anti-Slavery Society.

1842—Frederick Douglass, Jr. is born.

1844—Charles Redmond Douglass is born.

1841–45—Douglass lectures for the Massachusetts Anti-Slavery Society.

1845—Douglass publishes his first book, *Narrative of the Life of Frederick Douglass, Written By Himself*.

1845—Douglass sails to England and stays until March 1847. Meanwhile, in the states, English Quakers negotiate with Auld to buy his freedom. Anna and the children remain at home in Massachusetts.

1847—Douglass returns to the U.S. and begins a lecture tour. He starts *The North Star*, his abolitionist news-paper, in Rochester, New York. The first issue appears on December 3, 1847.

1847–48—Douglass sends Rosetta to Albany to be schooled by the Mott sisters, Abigail and Lydia, who run a small, integrated school in their home.

Spring, 1848—Anna and the boys join Douglass in Rochester in March. Rosetta moves from Albany to Rochester later that spring.

July, 1848—Douglass attends the convention of women's rights leaders in Seneca Falls, New York.

August, 1848—Douglass enrolls Rosetta in Miss Tracy's Female Seminary, a private white girls' school near their house.

September, 1848—Rosetta goes to the first day of school at Miss Tracy's. After being isolated for two weeks, she is expelled. Again, Douglass sends her to the Motts' home school in Albany. Douglass puts pressure on the Rochester public schools to integrate.

March 22, 1849—Annie Douglass is born.

March 30, 1849—Douglass prints a "Letter to H. G. Warner" in *The North Star*.

1851—Douglass disagrees with William Lloyd Garrison, and they part company.

1853–54—Rosetta, Charles, and Lewis Douglass attend Rochester Public School, District #13.

1854—Rosetta attends Oberlin College Ladies' Preparatory Department.

1855—Douglass publishes his second book, *My Bondage and My Freedom*.

1857–59—Rosetta teaches in Philadelphia and then in Salem, New Jersey. Annie Douglass is finally allowed to attend the public school in the Douglass's neighborhood.

1859—Accused of helping John Brown in his raid on a fort in Harper's Ferry, Virginia, Douglass flees to England, where he lectures.

1860—Annie dies of scarlet fever. Douglass returns home.

1861—The Civil War breaks out.

1862—Rosetta moves to Philadelphia and teaches school there.

1863—Rosetta meets and marries Nathan Sprague, a Union soldier. Rosetta attends Salem Normal School in New Jersey by day and teaches at night, living with relatives of her mother, Uncle Perry and Aunt Lizzie.

1863–64—Frederick Douglass recruits over one hundred New York "colored" volunteers, including Charles and Lewis Douglass, to serve in the 54th Massachusetts.

1864—Douglass meets with Lincoln on at least two occasions.

April 9, 1865—The Civil War ends.

1865-72—Rosetta and Nathan settle in Rochester. For seven years, they move in and out of the Douglass household as Nathan struggles to support the family. He and Rosetta have six children: Annie (who dies young), Harriet, Estelle, Frederika, Rosabelle, and Herbert.

1872—While Nathan and Rosetta are living in the Douglass home on South Avenue in Rochester, the home is burned to the ground. Police suspect arson. Douglass and Anna relocate to Washington, D.C.

1874—Douglass becomes president of Freedman's Savings and Trust.

1877—Douglass becomes U.S. Marshall.

1880—Douglass is appointed recorder of deeds for Washington, D.C.

1881–2—Douglass writes and publishes his third autobiography, *Life and Times of Frederick Douglass*.

1882—Anna Douglass dies. Rosetta publishes a pamphlet about her mother, "My Mother as I Recall Her."

1884—Douglass marries Helen Pitts.

1889—Douglass becomes American consul-general to Haiti.

1891—Douglass resigns the post in Haiti and comes home to Cedar Hill, his second home near Washington, D.C.

1892—Douglass publishes a revision of *Life and Times of Frederick Douglass*.

February 20, 1895—Frederick Douglass dies.

1906—Rosetta Douglass Sprague dies.

Author's Note

I worked from extensive, primary and secondary sources to tell this story, using fictional elements and educated guesses where facts were missing, writing in the voice of Rosetta, and working from the facts that are known.

Primary Sources

Frederick Douglass, open letter "To H. G. Warner," published in *The North Star* on March 30, 1849. This letter is found by date in either Philip S. Foner, ed., *The Life and Writings of Frederick Douglass*, 5 vols. (New York: International Publishers, 1950-1975), or in John Blassingame, ed., *The Frederick Douglass Papers*, 5 vols. to date, further letters to be published in forthcoming volumes (New Haven: Yale University Press).

Douglass retold the story of Rosetta's first days in school years later in his third autobiography, *The Life and Times of Frederick Douglass* (Hartford: Park, 1881), pp. 331-334. This book was republished in a replicated edition in 2001 by Digital Scanning, Inc., Scituate, MA 02066 (www.digitalscanning.com); trade paperback ISBN 1-58218-366-X; hardcover ISBN 1-58218-367-8; e-book ISBN 1-58218-365-1.

Writing to Amy Post of Rochester, Douglass mentions "a dear meeting with my own dear Rosetta" as he visited the Mott sisters, in a letter of September 29, tentatively assigned a date of 1847, but it may be 1848. In this letter he asks that Anna come to the Motts by train, in order to see Rosetta and to attend the upcoming Colored National Convention with him, an annual event held in Syracuse. Nothing else in the letter pins down a year. See "Letter 83," University of Rochester, Frederick Douglass project at www.lib.rochester.edu/rbk/douglass/horantr83.stm. The note by Eric Horan erroneously identifies the Motts referred to as Lucretia and James, rather than Abigail and

Lydia. Lucretia often visited her sisters-in-law, but she lived in Philadelphia, while the two sisters lived just outside Albany and very close to the train. The Mott sisters of Albany were close friends of Amy Post's, Douglass's friend and confidante in Rochester.

Letters exchanged between Douglass and his children are found in Mark A. Cooper, ed., *Dear Father: Letters to Frederick Douglass from His Children*, published in paperback by Fulmore Press in 1990. The volume contains several letters by Rosetta, the earliest from 1859. Other letters by Rosetta exist in manuscript and are held in the Library of Congress rare manuscript collection. One of these, which Rosetta wrote in 1860, is reprinted in this book.

The Douglass children and their educations are mentioned in Douglass's "Letter to His Old Master," written in 1846 while he was in England, published in *The North Star* in September 1848 and also reprinted as back matter in the second autobiography, *My Bondage and My Freedom* (New York: Dover, 1969). A replication of the original text of 1855 was published by Miller, Orton and Mulligan of New York and Auburn, pp. 421-428.

See also Rosetta Douglass Sprague, "My Mother as I Recall Her," pamphlet, published in Washington, 1900. (This source does not mention her first days of school, nor does it explain that her mother could not read.)

Secondary Sources

Further research on Rosetta's education is noted in John Blassingame et al., eds., *Frederick Douglass Papers*, vol. 2, 1847-1854 (New Haven: Yale University Press, 1982), p. 534n. Here Blassingame indicates that Rosetta went back to Albany after her expulsion in Rochester. Blassingame includes notes on the history of integrating the Rochester schools. Blassingame pieced together from unpublished letters and other documents that Rosetta was sent back to Albany in September 1848. Lacking direct primary evidence in Douglass's key narratives, I infer that other unpublished letters and documents underlay the conclusion by Blassingame.

William S. McFeely, *Frederick Douglass* (New York: W.W. Norton, 1990), pp. 331-334, retells the incident with details of context.

Dickson Preston, *Young Frederick Douglass: The Maryland Years* (Baltimore: Johns Hopkins, 1980), traces Douglass's heritage and his education as a child, until he ran away from Maryland in 1838. Preston shows the incomes of Douglass and his masters, the prices of slaves on the Eastern Shore at the time Douglass's master caught him trying to run away, and more facts about his mother and grandmother. The income (twenty dollars per month) of Thomas Auld as a ship captain and the fates of the other slaves originally owned by Aaron Anthony shed particular light on Douglass's trials as a rented slave earning more than his master's previous incomes. Preston traces the Bailey family tree in Maryland as far back as the 1700s.

Rochester April 2[0]
Friday morn[ing]

Dear Aunt Harriet—

Your kind and sympathizing letter was handed [me] this morning and very happy [was] I to receive it. I am now left alone being the only sister again, my loneliness at times I cannot describe. [My] darling sister is now an angel and happiness in Heaven is to me a consolation and I would not—if I could—see her back to earth amidst all the sorrow and suffering that we are to bear. [Some]times I feel as if I could only see her blithe and lively on earth once more and then the thought comes to console me that she is infinitely happier [in] Heaven than she ever was here or would have been she has gone to [Heaven] where love is the same for the b[est]

A letter from Rosetta to her aunt Harriet, 1860. Note her formal handwriting.

in sorrow we have no reason
suppose that it will not end in
if we walk in the paths of love
& duty to God. I have just asked
ther what I should say for her
d she as she is unable to write will
w my letter to be an answer for both,
sends her love to you and Tillie
as heartily as my self for your sym.
hizing letter, she also wishes me to tell
to please come and bring your
st daughter with you which I sup-
se is Tillie, she is not very well
I being quite feeble though about
house. Mother requests me to say
that if you desire to write a page
to father do so and send
to us and we will mail un-
cover with ours. Please write
s as soon as possible and as
us of your determination to
, Love to Cousin Matilda and
other little cousin whose name I

95

Photos and Other Documents

The University of Rochester provided the artist with photos of Rochester sites that are mentioned in the story, especially the house on Alexander Street, before it burned down on June 2, 1872. I was unable to locate an original image of Miss Tracy's Female Seminary.

Thanks to Nancy Martin, archivist at The University of Rochester, I've learned that Rosetta's house in Rochester, as well as her grave, have recently been identified.

The Library of Congress provided the page from *The North Star* on page 75, and the letter from Rosetta Douglass to her aunt Harriet, 1860, on pages 94 and 95.

—Linda Walvoord